# Cosmo
## THE DODO BIRD™

# Cosmo
## THE DODO BIRD™

Cosmo is a dodo bird, a unique species that lived on Earth 300 years ago. Cosmo lived with his family and beloved friends on the island of Mauritius, a paradise isolated from the world known to man.

When the first humans arrived on the island, the dodos' environment changed vastly, and it wasn't long before almost all of the dodos completely disappeared.

Now, Cosmo is the last of his kind on Earth.

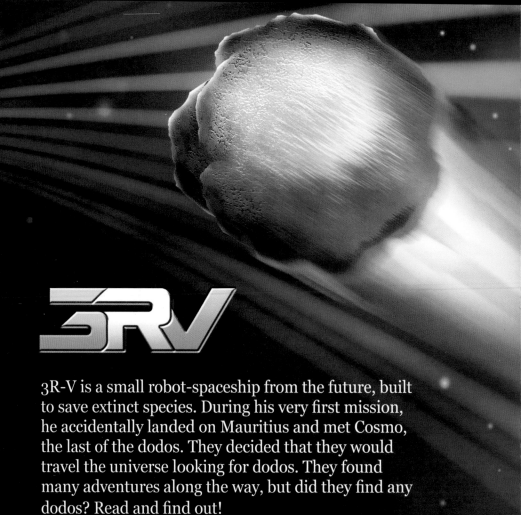

# 3RV

3R-V is a small robot-spaceship from the future, built to save extinct species. During his very first mission, he accidentally landed on Mauritius and met Cosmo, the last of the dodos. They decided that they would travel the universe looking for dodos. They found many adventures along the way, but did they find any dodos? Read and find out!

Originally published as *Les Aventures de Cosmo le dodo: La Tempête II*
by Origo Publications, POB 4 Chambly, Quebec J3L 4B1, 2008

Copyright © 2009 by Racine et Associés
Concept created by Pat Rac.
Editing and Illustrations: Pat Rac
Writing Team: Joannie Beaudet, Neijib Bentaieb, François Perras, Pat Rac

English translation copyright © 2011 by Tundra Books
This English edition published in Canada by Tundra Books, 2011
75 Sherbourne Street, Toronto, Ontario M5A 2P9

Published in the United States by Tundra Books of Northern New York,
P.O. Box 1030, Plattsburgh, New York 12901

Library of Congress Control Number: 2010928802

**Library and Archives Canada Cataloguing in Publication**
Pat Rac, 1963-
[Tempête II. English]
The chain reaction / Patrice Racine.

(The adventures of Cosmo, our hero of the enviroment)
Translation of: La tempête II.
For ages 8-11.
ISBN 978-1-77049-244-8

I. Title. II. Title: Tempête II. English. III. Series: Pat Rac, 1963- .
Adventures of Cosmo, our hero of the environment.

PS8631.A8294T44313 2011      jC843'.6      C2010-904300-6

We acknowledge the financial support of the Government of Canada through the Book Publishing
Industry Development Program (BPIDP) and that of the Government of Ontario through the
Ontario Media Development Corporation's Ontario Book Initiative. We further acknowledge the
support of the Canada Council for the Arts and the Ontario Arts Council for our publishing program.

ONTARIO ARTS COUNCIL
CONSEIL DES ARTS DE L'ONTARIO

*For more information on the international rights,
please visit www.cosmothedodobird.com*

Printed in Mexico

1 2 3 4 5 6    16 15 14 13 12 11

MIX
Paper from
responsible sources
FSC® C101537

# For all the children of the world

# THE ADVENTURES OF

# COSMO
## THE DODO BIRD
™

# THE CHAIN REACTION

TUNDRA BOOKS

# Table of Contents

*The adventure continues. . .*

# Prologue

I'm Cosmo the dodo bird. While living on the traveling planet, my friends and I found a mysterious object that fell from the sky. At first we thought it was a fireball, but we were wrong. We soon discovered it was a remote control device with amazing powers.

The buttons on it could change the climate! If we pressed the button with the picture of a raincloud, it rained. The button with the snowflake made it snow. The button with the sun – well, you get the idea.

Everybody was excited about the possibilities, and everybody wanted to use the remote control.

The two-heads often squabbled with itself, so when it got the remote, the right head made it snow over the left head, and Left made it rain over Right. Both heads caught colds. When Diggs snuck off to the beach instead of helping Fabrico do the cleaning, Fabrico sent clouds to spoil the sunny day. Worst of all, when Diggs seized the device, he decided to use its powers to rule the planet. I just wanted to bring back the sun.

Before that the climate had been nicely balanced with the right amount of sunshine, rain, warmth, and cold.

But once we started meddling with the weather, that balance was destroyed, and Nature objected. An enormous storm loomed, threatening to wreck everything. The planet began to experience a disaster that could have destroyed it.

Fortunately, before that could happen, a tornado swept past and I threw the remote into the center of it. The tornado went spinning away, taking the dangerous instrument with it. Our planet was saved, but black clouds still covered the sky. . . .

CHAPTER ONE

# Explosion

I did a happy dance once the remote control was gone. But not everyone shared my joy.

"*Grrr!* How can I become rich and powerful without that remote control?" growled Diggs.

"Don't be so selfish, Diggs," I told him. "We were doing terrible damage with that thing. Who knows what might have happened if we'd kept on trying to change the climate!"

I'm not sure if Diggs heard me because the wind had picked up. Before I could repeat myself, I noticed that Diggs was staring at something behind me, his eyes wide with fear. Even his pet lizard looked frightened. I peeked over my shoulder. The tornado that had sucked up the remote control had circled back and was growing larger before our very eyes!

"Duck!" cried Diggs, as a large branch snapped off a tree.

Diggs and I dived to the ground. The branch left us with a few scratches and scrapes, but no broken bones. Above our heads, the black clouds whirled and twisted. I looked around for my friends.

The two-heads leaned into the wind, and, with all its strength, made its way to shelter behind a rock. Fabrico gripped 3R-V's arm with one hand, and with the other he clutched his small umbrella. 3R-V calmly scanned the clearing to make sure we were all safe and sound.

I waved at my trusty friend. "3R-V, I'm over here!"

3R-V started toward me with Fabrico clinging tightly to his arm. Just then, another blast of wind and sand forced me to close my eyes. Diggs wasn't fast enough.

"Aaaah! My eyes are full of sand!" he cried.

The tornado was advancing. I was helping Diggs wipe his eyes, when we heard an awful sound.

A tree had been uprooted by the howling wind. It tottered over us.

"Diggs, look out!"

"What? What? What! I can't see!"

I shoved Diggs as hard as I could, just in time. The tree crashed down right between the two of us.

The tornado was destroying everything in its path. What was happening to the traveling planet that had become our home?

As I tried to get to my feet, 3R-V arrived and offered me a steady hand. Then he jumped over the tree trunk and scooped Diggs and his pet lizard into his arms before turning into the wind. He got us to the rock where the two-heads had already found shelter.

I thought about both of the planets we'd visited – was it only a few days ago? – where nothing had survived. Was our planet about to become as desolate? What would be our fate?

A streak of lightning flashed across the sky.

# CHAPTER TWO

# Fabrico's Flight

We all huddled together. Protected from the wind, we thought about our situation. 3R-V risked a look.

"The tornado has doubled in size! It's worse than ever!"

"What are we going to do?!" asked the right head.

"We can take refuge in my cave!" offered Diggs.

"It will be impossible to reach. The tornado's sucking up everything in its path," warned the left head.

"That might be true, but I'm afraid we'll have to try. Even this rock might come loose in the wind. We can't stay here much longer!" added 3R-V.

"It's the end of us," groaned Diggs.

Fabrico wasn't ready to give up. "I have an idea!" he shouted.

In his excitement, the purple fellow waved his arms. His umbrella was immediately pulled from his hand and sucked up by the tornado.

"Oh, no!" he cried. We all knew how much Fabrico loved that umbrella.

The umbrella twirled and danced gracefully for a moment. Then it disappeared into the swirling funnel.

"My marvellous umbrella! What can I do?" he cried.

"I'm afraid you'll have to forget about it, Fabrico!" said 3R-V. "It's too late to get it back."

Fabrico looked forlorn.

"You said you had a great idea." 3R-V reminded him.

"What?" Fabrico was still thinking about his umbrella.

"You said that you had an idea!"

"Look!" Fabrico exclaimed, his eyes bright. "There it is!" The umbrella twisted past.

"No, Fabrico!" I cried. "Don't!"

But before we could stop him, Fabrico dashed out from behind the rock and threw himself into the tornado. He looked like he was swimming in air, determined to reach his tiny treasure. Branches, leaves, and clumps of dirt whirled around him. Fabrico dodged them all with surprising skill.

"Fabrico's pretty agile!" I was impressed, even though I was worried about him.

"Dodo feathers! Dumb is more like it!" said Diggs.

Faster and faster, Fabrico dodged the debris. 3R-V plodded steadily toward him, despite the howling wind.

"Give me your hand, Fabrico!" he yelled.

Fabrico ignored him. He was a whisker away from the umbrella. At last, he grabbed it.

"I have you!" He gave a happy shout, but his joy was short lived. The tornado had him trapped in the whirlwind. "H . . . el . . . p!" he yelled.

The swirling wind had grown too strong, even for 3R-V. He couldn't get any nearer. The funnel abruptly shifted direction, and spun away from us, taking Fabrico and his precious umbrella with it.

"Fabrico!" we cried, but it was no use.

Our friend had disappeared into the black storm.

# CHAPTER THREE

# Through the Fog

I struggled out from behind the rock.

"Why on the traveling planet are you leaving our shelter?" asked Diggs.

"Fabrico is in danger! We have to help him."

"What about the storm?"

The sky was hidden by low dark clouds that practically brushed against our heads. Thunder rumbled in the distance. Then, as suddenly as it had arrived, the wind died. The air became heavy, making it hard to breathe. When lightning briefly lit up the sky, I caught sight of the tornado on its terrible path.

But none of that mattered. All I cared about was saving Fabrico. "3R-V, we have to go after him," I said firmly, even though I was shaking inside.

"What a dodo!" Diggs snorted.

But the two-heads understood the situation and followed me, leaving Diggs and his lizard shivering on their own.

Diggs had no choice but to call a half-hearted "Wait for me! I'm coming, too."

I ran as fast as I could to catch up with the tornado. Everything had turned suddenly quiet – too quiet. All I could hear were my footsteps.

I was surrounded by heavy fog, but I refused to let it stop me.

"Slow down, Cosmo," 3R-V called, his voice muffled by the fog. "We can't see anything!"

"You all have to hurry up. We must get through this thick fog, otherwise, we'll lose Fabrico's trail."

My friends didn't respond. Around me, everything was gray and silent.

"Left and Right? Diggs? 3R-V?" I called nervously.

Nothing. Alone in the fog, I shuddered. My feathers were standing on end. I was so nervous that I began to hear strange noises and creaking sounds.

"Is that you, 3R-V?" I tried to stay calm, but a clap of thunder boomed overhead, making me jump. Lightning lit the blanket of fog. In the eerie light I saw a strange shadow.

Is it a monster, I wondered. I hope it doesn't see me! I stood motionless and terrified, hoping the fog would hide me.

Unfortunately, a breeze began to blow, scattering the mist until only a few wisps remained. I was stuck. It would only take a few seconds for the monster to see me!

The fog lifted and to my great surprise, the "thing" wasn't a monster at all. Standing in front of me were my three friends – and the lizard!

"Thank goodness it's you! Did you see where the tornado went?" I asked eagerly.

"We lost sight of it," admitted 3R-V.

"Well, we have to find it!"

Diggs didn't move. He folded his arms across his chest. "I have a better idea," he growled. "Let's go to my cave where we'll be safe and sound until we're sure the storm is gone for good."

"Not without Fabrico! He's our friend."

"*Grrr!* It's his own fault that he's lost. He should never have gone after his silly umbrella!"

The wind was growing stronger. Lightning bolts began to strike the ground. Driving rain and uprooted trees flying about put us in danger once more. We all held fast to 3R-V as he plodded through the storm, like a shield in battle.

Abruptly, the wind stopped.

"Oof!" 3R-V stopped too.

In the brief lull I looked at the devastated landscape.

"Fabrico, where are you?" I shouted, though I knew it was hopeless.

I didn't see the enormous cloud forming above us, but the left head is scientific and notices everything.

ATCH!

# CHAPTER FOUR

# Short Circuit

My eyes were open, but I couldn't see much because dense smoke surrounded me. Small fires burned here and there.

"Friends?" I said weakly before a coughing fit made me double over. I felt a hand on my shoulder.

"Are you all right?" asked the right head.

I managed a hoarse "Yes, yes!"

"Is anyone hurt?" asked Left.

"No," grumbled Diggs.

The smoke slowly cleared. As I ruffled my feathers to shake off the ashes, the two-heads yanked me back. "Watch out! Look in front of you, Cosmo!"

A huge crater had been made by the lightning bolt and I had almost fallen into it. Worse than that, there was no trace of 3R-V.

Gingerly I made my way to the edge and peered in. Just as I feared, through a spiral of smoke, I spotted 3R-V lying at the bottom. The electric shock from the lightning had mangled the robot-ship's circuits.

"3R-V!"

No response. The broken little spaceship lay motionless on the ground.

"3R-V is hurt!" Tears rolled down my beak.

Diggs and the two-heads knelt beside me to see for themselves. Thunder rumbled in the distance, and the sky was still dark. Before I had time to worry about more stormy weather, a traveling-planet quake shook the ground. I jumped to my feet along with Diggs and the two-heads.

The quake went on and on. I was too scared to run, and anyway, there was no place to run to. A crack had formed in the ground, spreading toward me. I was helpless. In a moment I would be lying next to 3R-V at the bottom of the crater.

# CHAPTER FIVE

# At the Edge of the Chasm

Sure enough, the ground opened and I fell into the void. I flapped my stubby wings, even though they couldn't help me fly. I was about to crash head first, when I was pulled up short. A hand had grabbed my legs. It belonged to Diggs.

"*Grrr!* Cosmo, don't move!" Diggs grunted. "You certainly flirt with danger, don't you?"

Diggs teetered on the edge of the crater. His loyal lizard pulled on his feet, but she was too small to be of much use. I had stopped falling, but the wind was blowing me from side to side. Diggs's grasp was slipping in the driving rain. I was just a few fingers from a fatal fall.

"Diggs, where is the two-heads?" I asked desperately.

"On . . . the other side of . . . the fissure," puffed Diggs, straining to hold on to me.

"Don't panic!" called the right head.

"Hang on, Diggs. We'll find a vine. We can use it to reach you on your side of the fissure!" added the left head.

I tried to see the robot-ship below, but the effort made me dizzy. I closed my eyes. "Diggs, what about 3R-V?"

Diggs's voice was strained. "Forget him. . . . 3R-V is . . . not in great shape."

I blinked, trying to see through the rain. I wanted to shake my head, but I knew that if I moved at all, I risked falling. Gusts of wind hit me from all directions.

"What are those heads doing?!" I could tell from Diggs's voice that he was nearly exhausted and couldn't hold on much longer.

Just then I heard the heads: "Oh no!" they were crying.

"What's keeping you?" shouted Diggs with the last of his strength. Each head shouted a response, but they drowned one another out.

"I can't understand you!" yelled Diggs. "Just come help me!"

But I had been able to pick up a few of the heads' words and they frightened me: "Tsunami! Enormous! Water! Tidal wave!"

# CHAPTER SIX

# Making Waves

The two-heads thrashed around, trying to warn us, but Diggs and I could not see what was happening.

Suddenly, an immense wave engulfed us, and Diggs lost his hold on me.

I was swept away by the force of the water. The current tossed me against the chasm walls. I was bruised and battered, and I couldn't tell which way was up, so I hoped for the best, picked a direction, and tried to swim.

I couldn't hold my breath much longer. Time was running out for me. I had to have air – and soon!

My whole body trembled as I fought the urge to breathe in water.

As suddenly as it had come, the wave retreated. I struck a root that was sticking out from the rock face and wrapped my wings around it with my last ounce of strength. I spit out water and drew a deep breath. Below me, the wave had covered the bottom of the crater with water.

Diggs had been swept over to the other side of the crater. He was safe and sound with the two-heads.

"Cosmo!?" Both heads were calling me.

"There he is! He's hanging on to that root!" shouted Diggs.

Right called out, "Don't let go, Cosmo!"

"We'll save you," added Left.

I nodded. A cold rain had started to fall again. My breath made little puffs of steam.

# CHAPTER SEVEN

# Cold Sweat

It took a while to find 3R-V through the rain. Finally, I caught sight of a glass dome at the bottom of the chasm.

"3R-V!" I yelled. "Get up!"

The rain continued, but now it was mixed with snow in the bitter cold. My beak chattered.

"3R-V! 3R-V! 3R-V!" I called, over and over. There was no answer.

I tried to tighten my grip on the root, but my wings were frozen. I was slipping!

Frightened, I looked down. A layer of ice was forming on top of the water. If I fell now, my bones were sure to break.

I tried again. "3R-V! 3R-V!"

The robot-ship finally opened his eyes and saw me hanging from the root.

Valiantly, he tried to take off to save me, but he couldn't move.

"What . . ."

3R-V was stuck in the ice! Only his arms were free. He slapped the ice surface with all his strength, but it didn't break.

Meanwhile, I was freezing. I couldn't feel my toes anymore. I tried wiggling them to reassure myself that they were still there.

3R-V could see that the snow was falling more heavily than before, and he could tell that the wind had picked up.

"The storm is getting worse. Hold on, Cosmo."

3R-V tried with all his might to free himself from the ice, but it kept him anchored. He was a prisoner.

My wings were coated with ice. I was tired. The smallest movement could make me fall. I was about to give up when I heard a far-off rumble. Was it a drum? Was I hearing things?

The noise grew louder. It was another traveling-planet quake! It shook me loose from my perch. I fell into the void.

The wind hit me from every side. I closed my eyes. The drop seemed endless.

# CHAPTER EIGHT

# Step by Step

Then, with a jolt, I stopped. I had hit something, but what? I tested all the parts of my body: toes, wings, head. Everything worked. What had broken my fall? I opened an eye. It was 3R-V!

"I thought you were stuck in the ice . . ."

"The quake cracked the ice and I was able to get my feet out. When I saw you falling, I took off as fast as I could!"

My friend set me down by Diggs and the two-heads.

"Well done 3R-V!" shouted Left.

"Hurry! It's snowing harder." said Right.

The rain clouds had given way to clouds that were heavy with snow. 3R-V tried to shield us from the wind, but despite his efforts, we were all frozen stiff.

I was the first to speak. "Remember, we still have to find Fabrico!"

"It's too dangerous, Cosmo. Look at this blizzard!" said 3R-V.

"We'll all turn into ice statues," mused the right head.

I nodded, as much to shake the snow off my head, as to agree.

Reluctantly, I had to agree. "I guess we'll have to wait until the storm calms down before we look for Fabrico."

"If it ever calms down, that is," added the pessimistic Diggs.

"Diggs, your home is safe enough. After all, it's a cave," said Left. "Let's all take shelter there."

Our little group set off sadly in single file behind 3R-V. Though he made tracks for us to follow, every step was more difficult than the one before. The wind was icy. The snow and hail stung our faces. We could barely see a thing.

CHAPTER NINE

# A Harsh Winter

The snow was piling up so fast that we lost our bearings. Everything was white. We couldn't tell where the sky ended and the ground began. The way to Diggs's house seemed endless.

"I think we are going in circles," called Right.

"You're wrong. You never did have a sense of direction," responded Left.

"Huh! Know-it-all Left never makes a move without a road map," replied Right.

"I don't need a road map. I only carry it with me all the time to convince you of the best way."

"Stop it, heads! This is hard enough without having to put up with your quarrelling," shouted Diggs.

"Okay!" exclaimed the peace-keeper, 3R-V. "I'm going to do a fly-over of the area to pinpoint our exact location. Do you want to come with me, Cosmo?"

"Wait a minute, you two! Are you trying to abandon us in this storm?" asked Diggs.

"Of course not!" responded 3R-V, offended.

"3R-V, you go without me. I'll stay here with the others."

"But hurry back!" Diggs hastened to add.

3R-V took off into the white sky. Soon he had disappeared in the dense snowflakes.

I couldn't stop thinking about Fabrico. Was there any chance that he had survived the brutal storm? I shed a small tear. It turned into a little ice cube.

We stood frozen in the grip of the winter that had come to the traveling planet.

"I know. Let's dance!" said Right.

"Why would we do that?" demanded Diggs.

"To warm us up!"

"That's a good idea, Right," I said.

"*Grrr*, I'd rather keep looking for my home instead of doing some silly dance," shouted Diggs as he set off alone.

I knew I had to stop him. "Don't go alone, Diggs. We should all stay together. 3R-V will return soon!"

"Diggs doesn't know how to dance! Diggs doesn't know to dance!" teased the two-heads.

Suddenly, a snowball struck Right in the face.

"That will teach you to laugh at me," shouted Diggs.

Right and Left took turns throwing snowballs at Diggs.

"Take that, Grumpy Gus," they yelled.

Diggs rushed at the two-heads but it jumped out of the way. It tripped and began to slide down a steep slope, gathering snow as it went. Before we knew it, the two-heads had turned into a big snowball rolling down the hill.

"Ha, ha, ha! At least we've found something amusing about all this winter," chuckled the two-heads.

Diggs rolled down the slope too, but was stopped abruptly by an object sticking up through the snow.

"Hey, I know what that is! It's our telescope." yelled Right.

"You're right, Right," said Left. "At last we have a landmark!"

Then, 3R-V returned.

"Good work! You saw the same thing I did from the air."

As soon as 3R-V landed, I climbed aboard. We
descended the slope and called to the others.

"Come on! Diggs's cave is close by!"

"Wait for us!" cried the right head.

# CHAPTER TEN

# After-Effects

The two-heads' masterpiece was in pieces. I was examining the damage when I heard both heads shout, "Oh no!"

I turned to see them digging frantically through the snow.

"Why are you digging . . ." Then I realized we were in the two-heads' field of flowers.

"Oh dear! The hope flowers!"

The two-heads uncovered a flower, its petals encased in ice. They bent over the frozen blossom.

Yet another quake shook the traveling planet. The snow clouds were giving way to big black clouds. A fresh storm was brewing. We'd learned enough to know what was coming next. 3R-V took charge.

"Quick! Everyone to the cave!" he ordered.

We ran toward Diggs's house. Many obstacles blocked our path: uprooted tree trunks, cracks in the ground, thick and melting snow. But we finally arrived at the cave, only to find something amazing.

The cave entrance was completely clear of snow. Beside the opening stood a jaunty snowman.

"What's this? There must be someone here." Diggs rushed into his home, the rest of us on his heels.

"Hello, my friends! You certainly took your time getting here!"

"Fabrico! Fabrico! Fabrico! Fabrico! Fabrico!"
Everyone took a turn greeting him.

"What . . . How . . ." I stopped trying to figure it out and
smiled at the sight of Fabrico, safe and warm in front of
the cozy fireplace.

Outside the weather kept changing back and forth.

Lightning flashed across the sky. Snow changed to rain and rain changed to snow. "Nature is really raging!" said 3R-V. "We're lucky to have shelter at last."

A scratching sound sent Diggs to the door. His pet had always been an outdoor lizard. Diggs didn't want lizard tracks on his furniture. But the sight of his forlorn companion melted Diggs's heart.

"*Grrr!* Hurry up. Come on in!"

As Diggs held the door open, a jagged lightning bolt hit the cliff. Before anyone could do anything, enormous rocks blocked the doorway. The little lizard had disappeared under a pile of rubble.

"Lizardo!" Diggs cried, using his pet name for her. He dug frantically, and we all hurried to help him. But there was no sign of the little creature. "Lizardo, I'm sorry," wept Diggs.

# CHAPTER ELEVEN

# Waiting it Out

The storm raged outside: the wind howled and the rain pelted the cliff. We knew our efforts to save the lizard were useless. The mud between the rocks was hardening, turning the heap of rubble into a solid wall. Even 3R-V wasn't able to crack it. But Diggs wouldn't stop scratching at the wall.

Gently, I said "It is too late for her, Diggs."

"Little Lizardo!" he sobbed. "If only my helmet was working, I would be able to save her!"

Fabrico tried to console him. "Please stop crying, Diggs. We'll get you another lizard."

Diggs refused to be comforted. He wanted his own lizard back, and his grief rapidly turned into anger.

"What are you all doing in my home?" he demanded.

"I thought we agreed this was the safest place to wait out the storm!" said Fabrico.

"You didn't agree to anything, Fabrico. You were swallowed by the tornado!"

"Well . . . not exactly. That's to say . . . my extraordinary little object saved my life," Fabrico proudly unfurled his small umbrella.

"Fabrico! No more of your stories," said the two-heads.

Fabrico flushed an angry red. "Stories, eh?! Let me tell you about my adventure!"

Fabrico began his tale. "I spun around in the tornado again and again and again and again . . .

"We get it! The tornado carried you away!" muttered Diggs.

After a short pout, Fabrico continued. "I was lost in that tornado with nothing but my little umbrella!" he said dramatically. "I shouted in every direction for help. I was desperate. Then my umbrella handle snagged a branch, pulling me out of the funnel and leaving me spinning around and around and –"

Diggs threw Fabrico a menacing look.

"I opened an eye. And then . . ." Fabrico stopped.

"Go on, go on!" demanded the two-heads.

Fabrico continued. "It was dreadful!"

"What are you talking about?" I asked impatiently.

"An enormous wave was coming straight at me!"

"The tsunami!" we cried, caught up again in Fabrico's story.

"What did you do?" asked Left.

Fabrico proudly raised his little umbrella. "I opened this and jumped. I floated on the waves like . . . like . . ."

"A star floating in space?" suggested the right head.

"More like a boat on water."

"Not a very original image," muttered Right.

The purple fellow rolled his eyes, imagining himself surfing on the waves, his umbrella under his feet. But his vision was cut short when Diggs threw him a look as cold as an iceberg. Fabrico shook himself and returned to his story.

"The wave suddenly froze. That's when I remembered our initial plan: to take shelter in Diggs's cave."

"I started walking, using my closed umbrella as a cane, but I was so cold! The wind and snow whipped me in the face. Suddenly, my umbrella opened, and . . . guess what!"

"You fell face-first into the snow!" Diggs said spitefully.

"No!" responded Fabrico. "Try again."

"We don't have the time for this," snapped Diggs.

"It seems to me that we have quite a bit of time," said 3R-V mildly. "Fabrico, go on. What happened next?"

After some coaxing, Fabrico continued. "The wind had taken hold of my wonderful umbrella and turned it into a sail! In a flash I had glided across the frozen lake. When I got to Diggs's cave, there wasn't anyone here. I waited and waited. It took you ages to arrive! What were you slowpokes doing?"

3R-V and I had to hold Diggs back.

"After all these adventures, we need a rest," I said, trying to make peace. Exhausted by the ordeals of the storm, we all sank into a dreamless sleep.

# CHAPTER TWELVE

# Another Day

We were warm and dry and well sheltered from the storm, but we knew we were still in trouble. The rock fall had imprisoned us in Diggs's cave. Without a way to leave, we would soon run out of food and water. I didn't want to think about what that would be like.

Our only hope was Diggs's helmet. If he could repair it so that the drill was working, he might be able to dig a hole in the wall of rubble and free us.

Diggs was the first to wake up the next morning. He went to his workshop, and by the light of a candle, he sat down at his table to repair his helmet.

"I'm missing a part. I need it to get this thing working again." Diggs muttered. "*Grrr!*"

Diggs's growling woke the rest of us. I hurried to the wall, pressed my ear against it, and heard that the storm was still raging outside.

Fabrico saw Diggs's candle and had an idea.

"We have fire," he cried. "Does anyone have marshmallows?"

We were all too sleepy to answer.

"Any sausages?" Fabrico tried again.

Again, nobody responded.

"Fire, fire, lovely fire!" sang the purple fellow.

"Be quiet, Fabrico!" ordered Diggs.

"My, my. Aren't we cranky!" said Fabrico. "What has you in such bad mood?"

Diggs sighed deeply. "Losing Lizardo," he said.

"That, and the devastated field of hope flowers," said the two-heads.

"Yes, and the storm that's ravaging everything," added 3R-V.

"Plus the end of the traveling planet," I added quietly.

"Don't exaggerate, Cosmo!" The left head chided me.

"Before the storm, 3R-V and I explored two other planets," I reminded the others.

"Those planets had suffered the ravages of a storm," explained 3R-V.

I described what we'd seen. "The lakes and rivers had dried up, the trees were all uprooted, the ground was cracked."

"It's all the fault of the remote control!" Diggs said.

"I think you're right," said Left.

Right spoke up. "Before that remote control fell from the sky we'd never seen weather like this."

"Blasted remote control!" Fabrico cried.

I hung my head. "Suppose it wasn't the remote control's fault? After all, we're the ones who used it unwisely."

"I think you'd better explain yourself," said the left head.

"I wanted the remote control to get rid of the clouds. I didn't pay attention to the signs that the traveling planet was sending us."

"And I used the remote control to play tricks on Diggs," admitted Fabrico

"You and I," said Left to Right, "used it to attack each other . . ."

" . . . without worrying about the impact on our poor planet!" finished an emotional Right.

We all turned to look at Diggs.

"What?!"

"Don't you have anything to say, Master Diggs?" Fabrico prodded.

Diggs produced a growl. "*Grrr!* Maybe I did use the remote control just a bit to acquire power," he admitted. "Now, be quiet, all of you! Fixing my helmet requires total concentration."

CHAPTER THIRTEEN

# Times are Hard

The days passed slowly. Diggs worked non-stop on his helmet, while Fabrico asked over and over, "Is it fixed yet?"

"No!"

"Okay. . . . Is it repaired now?"

"No!"

"Diggs, have you –"

"*Grrr!* As soon as it is fixed, I will get us out of here! Stop asking questions!"

"Okay," said Fabrico. But a few moments later, he was at it again.

"Is it fixed yet?"

"*Grrr!*" was the only reply.

The rest of us spent our time listening to the sounds of the storm – the wind howling, the rain drumming on the rocks, the thunder rumbling, and the ground trembling. The storm on the traveling planet was never-ending. We were all tired and bored.

Every day was the same. Diggs worked on his helmet. Fabrico peppered him with questions or played thumb wars with himself. The left head wrote notes. The right head composed poetry. 3R-V and I organized the cleaning and cooking.

By the end of a week, a gloom had settled over everyone. Even Fabrico became quieter with each passing day. Our food supply was nearly exhausted, and we had to reduce our portions. I often heard my friends' stomachs rumbling. 3R-V was the only one who didn't suffer from the lack of food. We allowed ourselves only three sips a day of the water that leaked, drop by drop, through a small hole in the wall.

I couldn't wait for the storm to end and for Diggs to repair his helmet!

It was hard to know when it was night because inside the cave, it was always dark except for the flicker of candles. There were no suns or moons to tell us the time. There were no sounds, except from the storm outside, and our stomachs inside.

I slept on the hard ground, dreaming the same dream, night after night. In my dream, the other dodos and I frolicked in clear blue waters under the comforting sun of Mauritius. I felt happy, free, and safe.

One night I awoke to the sound of crying. Everyone was asleep except for the right head.

"What's wrong, Right?"

"I finished my poem," Right replied, handing me a piece of paper. I squinted to read it in the dim candlelight.

In the heart of the storm,
My weeping eyes see all:
The trees, the lakes, the flowers,
Ruined. All of them ruined!

The wind howls, the ground trembles, the sky cries!

In the heart of the storm,
My weeping eyes see everything:
The earth, the air, the planet,
Wounded. Helpless. Defeated!

The wind howls, the ground trembles, the sky cries!

In the heart of the storm,
My weeping eyes see everyone:
The stubborn, the foolish, the greedy,
Guilty. All guilty of insane neglect!

And still the wind howls, the ground trembles, the sky cries!

Is this the end of our beautiful planet? Unbearable tragedy!

I shook my head. "Don't give up, Right. Our planet's environment was healthy before we tampered with it. Maybe we can reverse the damage somehow."

"I don't have much hope," Right sighed. "You saw how the two other planets were destroyed by the storm."

I fell silent. A few minutes later, Right dozed off. I tried to sleep too, but my head was full of ideas bumping into each other. Was this really the end of the traveling planet?

# CHAPTER FOURTEEN

# A Brutal Awakening

It was 3R-V who woke us.

"Listen!" he ordered.

"To what?" asked Fabrico.

"Don't you hear?"

"What? What? What? I don't hear anything," Fabrico said.

"Precisely!" exclaimed 3R-V. "There's no wind or rain!"

I leapt to my feet. "The storm is over!"

"Hurray!" we cried together, dancing joyfully around the cave.

"What are you so happy about? Without my helmet to drill us out of here, we are still prisoners. Grrr!"

Our joy vanished. Diggs was right. How would we ever get out of here?

"Move away from the wall!" exclaimed 3R-V. "I'm going to break it down!"

"Wait!" grumbled Fabrico. "My fabulous little umbrella might get us out of here."

"Move, Fabrico!" Diggs ordered.

"Just listen to me!" insisted Fabrico.

But nobody paid any attention to him. We were completely focused on 3R-V. He was our only hope.

The robot-ship prepared to charge. At the far end of the room, he aimed directly at the wall of stones and revved his engines to full power. He flew straight at the wall, but the only result was a loud thud, a dazed robot, and a wall that still blocked our escape. The robot-ship's attempt had failed. If 3R-V couldn't get us out, who could?

"Well! That didn't work. Now it's my turn," said Fabrico. "Allow me to demonstrate the uses of my wonderful umbrella."

With that, he stuck his umbrella into a crack in the rubble. Fabrico rubbed his hands and firmly gripped the handle. Then he leaned on it with all his strength as if it were a lever. The rocks didn't budge, but the umbrella bent nearly in two.

With a loud Snap! the umbrella shattered. Pieces of it flew all over the cave. One of them landed on the table near Diggs.

"Well, look at this! It's exactly what I've needed all along!" he exclaimed.

Diggs took the bit of metal and inserted it into his helmet's mechanism. Carefully, he entered a code. It worked! Before our eyes, his helmet transformed into a drill!

I was thrilled. "Diggs, your helmet is repaired! We can leave the cave!"

Without wasting a moment, Diggs drilled through the wall of rock and mud that blocked our way out.

"Hurray!" we shouted. "Fabrico, you were right after all!! Your fabulous little umbrella did save the day!"

BANG!

We filed out of Diggs's cave, squinting in the bright light. I had been behind the two-heads, and when it stopped suddenly, I bumped into it.

"The . . . the . . . the . . . traveling planet!" The left head stuttered.

"A ravaged beauty, scattered into a thousand pieces," wailed Right.

We walked on the traveling planet, stunned by the ruined landscape.

We nearly wept when we reached the lake and saw what the storm had done. The beach was gone; the ground around the lake was soggy. The water was murky and clogged with debris.

In silence, we left the lake and entered what had once been a cool, green forest. Most of the trees were uprooted. I touched a trunk, and the bark crumbled beneath my fingers. Everything was covered in a thick layer of dried mud.

In the distance, even the highest mountain had not been spared by the storm. Mudslides scarred the mountainsides.

I couldn't bear the sight of it. "The traveling planet has been totally destroyed."

"Like the last two planets that you and I explored," added 3R-V.

"I'm afraid we'd better prepare to leave our traveling planet," said Diggs.

The two-heads wailed: "Leave home? Never!"

Fabrico was crying. "Where will I go? You . . . you . . . you are my only family!"

"The traveling planet is no longer viable," said Diggs firmly. "The storm destroyed everything!"

"I'm afraid Diggs is right," 3R-V added.

Together, the heads were stubborn: "No!" they cried together.

I understood how they felt because I, too, had grown to love the traveling planet with its green forest, clear lake, dazzling orange sky – and my comfy nest.

I couldn't let all of that go so easily. "Let's not give up on the planet yet. Maybe we can restore it!"

"Nonsense!" protested Diggs. "The lake's finished. There are no more trees. The ground is parched."

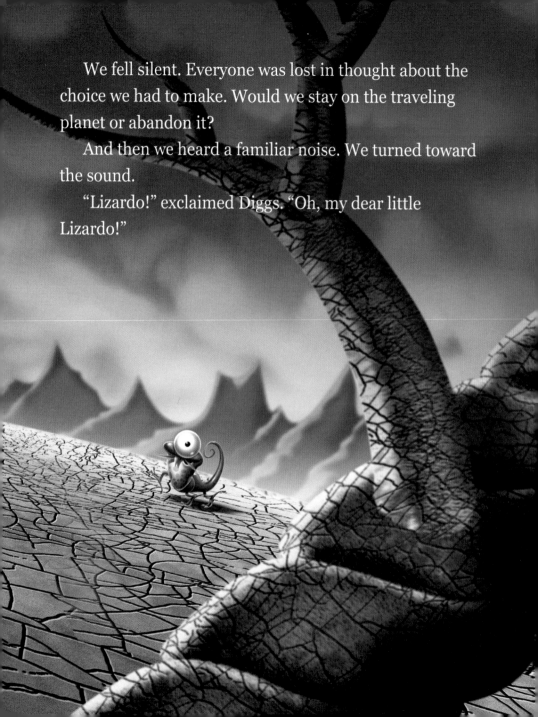

We fell silent. Everyone was lost in thought about the choice we had to make. Would we stay on the traveling planet or abandon it?

And then we heard a familiar noise. We turned toward the sound.

"Lizardo!" exclaimed Diggs. "Oh, my dear little Lizardo!"

# Against All Odds

I was astonished. Diggs's little lizard was alive! She ran to him, her tail wriggling in every direction. She leapt into the air and Diggs caught her in mid-flight.

"Lizardo, you missed me!" said a joyful Diggs.

"What does she have in her mouth?" demanded 3R-V.

I reached out to the lizard, but she growled, showing her pointed fang.

"Gently, Lizardo, gently," crooned Diggs. "You can't scare us with your one little fang."

Diggs hugged his pet once more, then he pulled himself together. "All right now, the cuddles are over! Show me what you have in your mouth. Give it to me. That's a good girl!"

The lizard did as she was told. She dropped a blade of grass into Diggs's hand.

"What do you want me to do with this?" asked Diggs.

"Lizardo, where did you pick that grass?" Right and Left were excited.

"*Grrrrrr!*" growled Lizardo, sounding very much like Diggs.

Diggs scratched her neck and tried again. "Show us where you found the grass growing."

The lizard jumped to the ground and scurried through the uprooted trees. We hurried after her. She came to a stop near the two-heads' telescope, which was half-buried in the ground.

Lizardo took a few steps and turned to look at Diggs. She flicked her tongue and seemed quite proud of herself.

"Is this it?" asked Diggs, irritated. "I don't see anything except mud and more mud!"

Just then, a ray of sun pierced the gray clouds and lit up the clearing. Little flowers were sprouting here and there.

"Look! It's the field of hope flowers!" I exclaimed.

"The hope flowers survived the storm!" cried the two-heads.

As Fabrico danced in delight through the field of flowers, the two-heads warned, "Don't crush the shoots!"

"Do you think I'm a klutz?" shouted Fabrico, right before he tripped on a root and fell head-first into a puddle.

"Ouch!" dozens of sweet voices cried.

"Who said that?" demanded Fabrico. "I can't see anything with this dirt in my eyes."

When he was finished wiping his face, Fabrico saw that he was nose to nose with some delicate hope flowers. "Look! The hope flowers are talking!"

We gathered around them.

"The traveling planet is coming back to life!" I said softly.

Inspired, the right head started another poem:

"After the storm, my eyes are clear. Now I can see everything.

The sun, the breeze, the flowers smiling – all for us!"

# Epilogue

In time, the sun shone brightly on the traveling planet. There was not a cloud in the clear orange sky. The breeze was warm and pleasant. Plants flourished again, turning the parched ground green. The traveling planet had found its natural balance once more.

Beside me, Fabrico sighed.

"What's bothering you, my friend?"

"All that cleaning gone to waste! To think that I had cleaned everything before the storm."

The two-heads, 3R-V, and I laughed.

"What's so funny? Everything is getting dirty!"

"We'll help you with the cleaning, Fabrico!"

"Really? You always find silly excuses not to help. 'We have to explore a new planet,' or 'I'm repairing a helmet,' or 'We're monitoring the telescope. Blah, blah, blah!'"

"There will be no excuses this time," I assured him. "We'll all help to keep the traveling planet clean, won't we, Diggs?"

Diggs was about to tiptoe away with his lizard by his side. Reluctantly, he stopped.

"*Grrr!*"

A few minutes later, everyone was hard at work. 3R-V hauled the tree trunks into the middle of the clearing. The two-heads polished the telescope. Fabrico removed the mud around the hope flowers with a toothbrush. Even Diggs did his part by sweeping the ground, while Lizardo cleaned his helmet with her tongue.

Feather duster in-hand, I paused to gaze at the sky above me and the awakening landscape around me. I didn't hear 3R-V approach.

"What are you thinking, Cosmo?"

"We nearly lost the traveling planet because everyone wanted to control the climate!"

"You're right. We had a close call. But together, we managed to overcome the storm."

I took a deep breath.

"Is something bothering you?" 3R-V asked.

"There's no trace of the remote control. I wonder were it is?"

3R-V thought for a moment. "Let's just hope that whoever finds it next is smarter than we were. . . ."

*The end!*